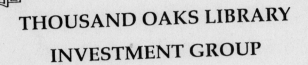

ROBIN BALLARD

Good-bye, House

Greenwillow Books, New York

For Nora

Pen and ink and watercolors were used
for the full-color art.
The text type is Helvetica Rounded.

Library of Congress Cataloging-in-Publication Data

Ballard, Robin.
    Good-bye, house / by Robin Ballard.
        p.   cm.
    Summary: A child says goodbye to the old house before
moving with Mama and Papa to a new home.
    ISBN 0-688-12525-5 (trade).
    ISBN 0-688-12526-3 (lib. bdg.)
    [1. Dwellings—Fiction.
2. Moving, Household—Fiction.]   I. Title
PZ7.B2125Gn   1994
[E]—dc20   93-252   CIP   AC

We are moving to a new house. All of our things are packed in boxes. Mama and Papa pile them up in the back of a big truck. I am sad to leave. I do not want to go. This is the only home I have ever known.

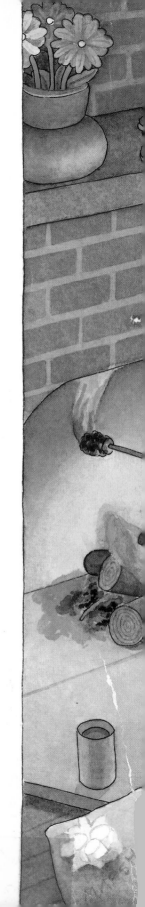

I said good-bye to the living
room and the fireplace full
of ashes from toasting
marshmallows.

I said good-bye to the
kitchen. My seat had been
right here, and Mama and
Papa sat over there.

I said good-bye to the bottom
cupboard. Cups, saucers, and
a teapot—and just enough
room for me and my guests.

I said good-bye to the
basement. It had been
Papa's workshop, where
he made my big bed.

I said good-bye to my room.
I picked out the color, and
Mama and I painted it
together.

I said good-bye to the marks
along my door. The first mark
is where I began, and now I
stand this tall.

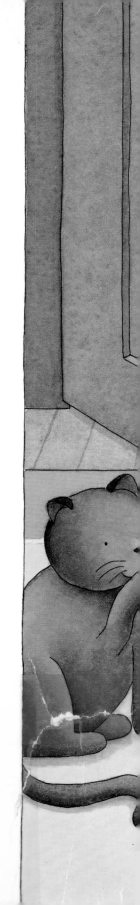

I said good-bye to the tree
that cast a shadow through
my window when I went to
sleep.

I counted the steps for the last time. Eight steps down the hall, then two to the left. I could find my way to the toilet when the house was dark.

I said good-bye to the bathroom and the small hole in the ceiling where the rain came in.

I said good-bye to Mama and Papa's room. I said good-bye to the sewing closet in the corner. Behind the doors Mama kept thread and cloth that she made into things for me to wear.

I hear Papa calling me. It is
time to go.
We say good-bye to the house.

As we drive away, I watch the house get smaller and smaller until it disappears. We are going to a new house.

I think I will like it here.